Toothamungus

Written by : Michelle Dass
Illustrated by : Kendy Joseph

Copyright © 2020 by Michelle Dass

All rights reserved. No part of this book may be reproduced, stored in a retrieval system, or transmitted in any form or by any means electronic, mechanical, photocopying, recording or otherwise, without the express written permission of the copyright holder.

ISBN-13: 978-0-9990577-3-5

To my son Jalen and all the readers of this book, thank you for giving my story a chance.

Toothamungus was a great white shark who lived deep beneath the Atlantic ocean. His name is a combination of his first name TOOTH, middle initial A., and his last name MUNGUS.

In the world of sharks, he was called Toothamungus. This name was given to him by his grandfather Kobemungus or Kob E. Mungus if we are being shark proper.

Toothamungus was strong and fast, but certainly not friendly. His attitude was due to the fact that he whistled and slurred his words when he spoke. These were consequences of his missing front teeth.

Good oral hygiene was a huge part of the Mungus family's daily lives.

The family consisted of Kobemungus (the head of the family), Ririmungus (grandmother), Meggiemungus (Mom), Michemungus (aunt), Jaymungus (brother), Meedamungus (sister) and Toothamungus.

They all flaunted beautiful smiles.

Munquis family

When Toothamungus was a pup (a baby shark), he was considered to have the best looking smile of all the Mungus family.

As he grew older, he excitedly took care of his teeth and gums.

He enjoyed brushing and flossing often.

Apart from having good oral hygiene, brushing and flossing, he also worked his arm muscles (biceps).

While Toothamungus enjoyed looking at his growing biceps and pearly white teeth, after some time, it became a chore for him.

You see, Toothamungus had about 300 teeth (WOW)............................arranged in many rows. That is a lot of teeth. He just got tired of brushing twice a day.

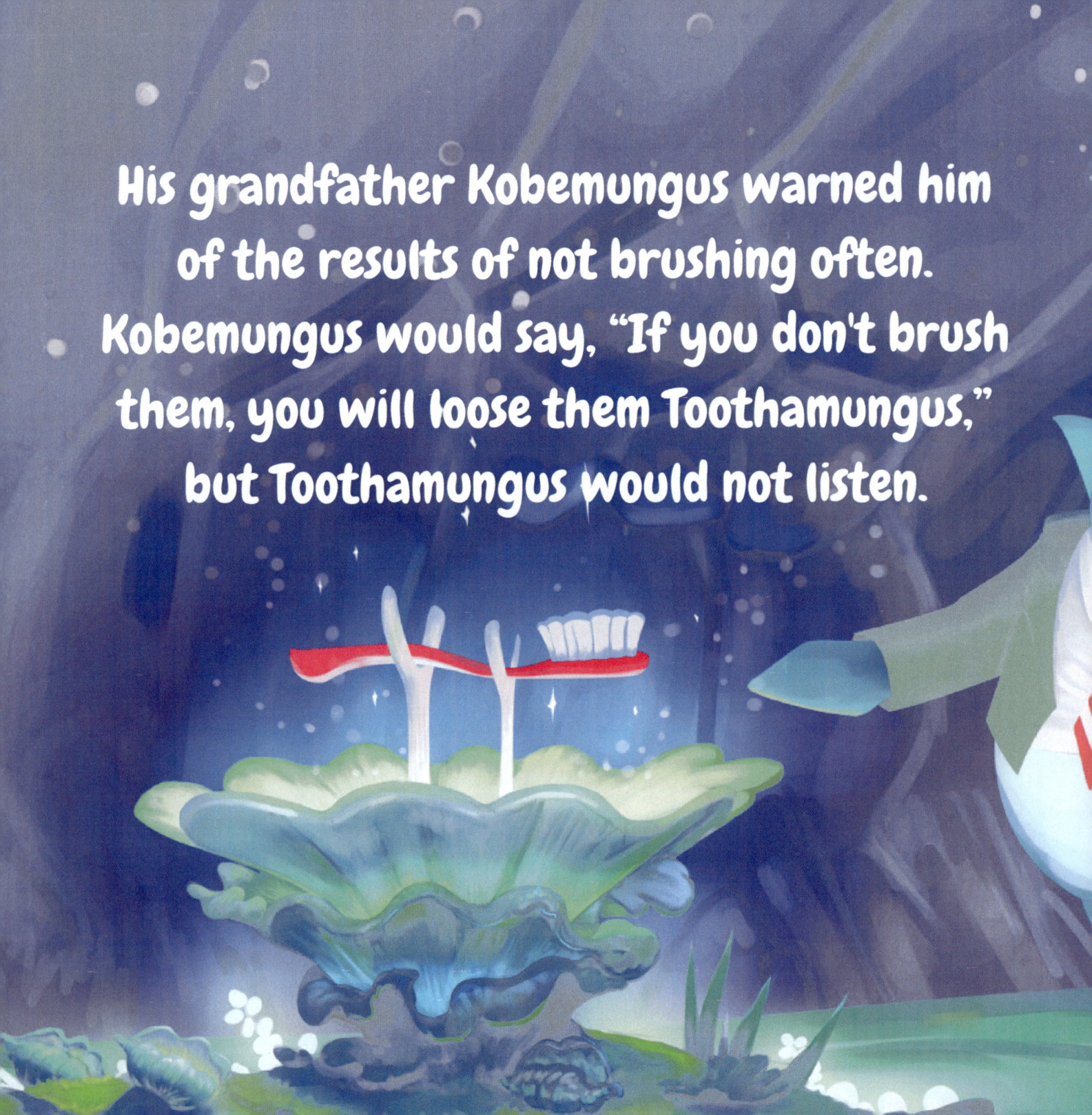

His grandfather Kobemungus warned him of the results of not brushing often. Kobemungus would say, "If you don't brush them, you will loose them Toothamungus," but Toothamungus would not listen.

He went from brushing and flossing twice per day to once per day, to............, well, let's just say he stopped taking care of his teeth.

As a result, Toothamungus began getting cavities and bad breath.

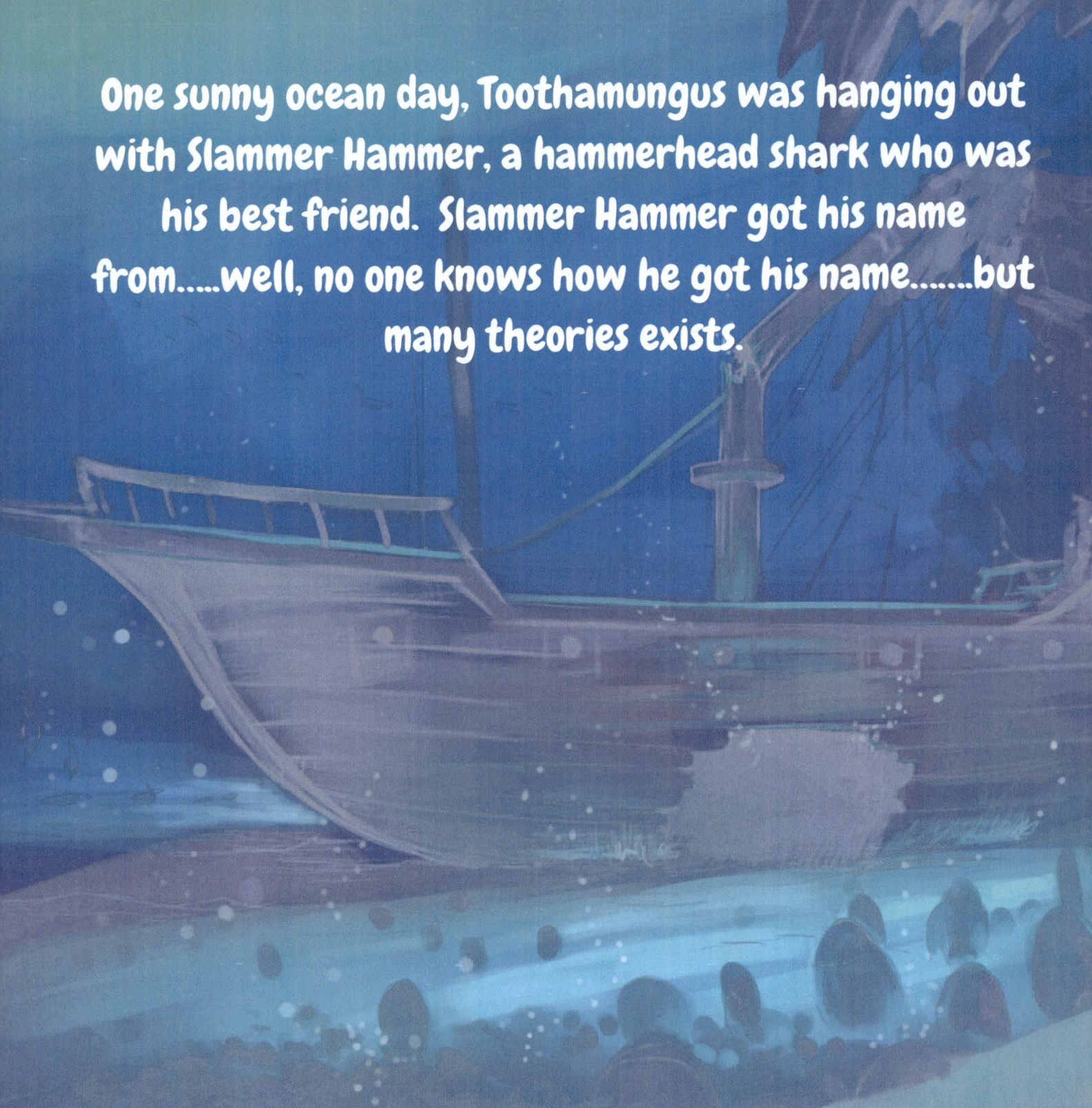

One sunny ocean day, Toothamungus was hanging out with Slammer Hammer, a hammerhead shark who was his best friend. Slammer Hammer got his name from…..well, no one knows how he got his name…….but many theories exists.

As the sharks hung out, joking around and making small talk, they started getting hungry. They decided to do some fishing in the nearby sunken ship.

Toothamungus immediately saw a fish he was interested in having for lunch. He began going after the fish. He chased the fish all through the sunken ship, up and down, inside and through its many doors.

The fish reached the anchor and toothamungus was confident that he would easily get his prey.

As he swam toward the anchor, he opened his mouth wide and bit down hard to finally catch the fish. However, instead of biting the fish, he bit the anchor. This resulted in several of his front teeth falling out.

You see, his teeth easily fell out because they were already weak from not being cleaned often.

Toothamungus was very disappointed. He was also embarrassed, his smile had changed significantly and he was still hungry.

He decided to meet back up with Slammer Hammer, who he found having lunch with Elton, a basking shark who feeds on microscopic plankton. He tried to hide the change in his smile – but not for long.

When they heard what happened to Toothamungus, they started laughing.

I told you to become a vegetarian, said Slammer Hammer. Now you will have to constantly whistle when you speak.

Later on that day, after a vulnerable Toothamungus told his family what had happened, he vowed to take care of his teeth.

The Mungus family enjoyed a group hug to mourn the loss of Toothamungus's missing teeth.

From that day forward Toothamungus started flossing and brushing again.

He decided to get a chain with an anchor pendant which serves as a reminder of the days when he felt lazy about taking care of his pearly whites.

What is your shark name?

List your first name and middle initial below.

_____ ____   MUNGUS!
First Name   Middle Initial

_____Mungus

Other Books by Michelle Dass

COMING SOON

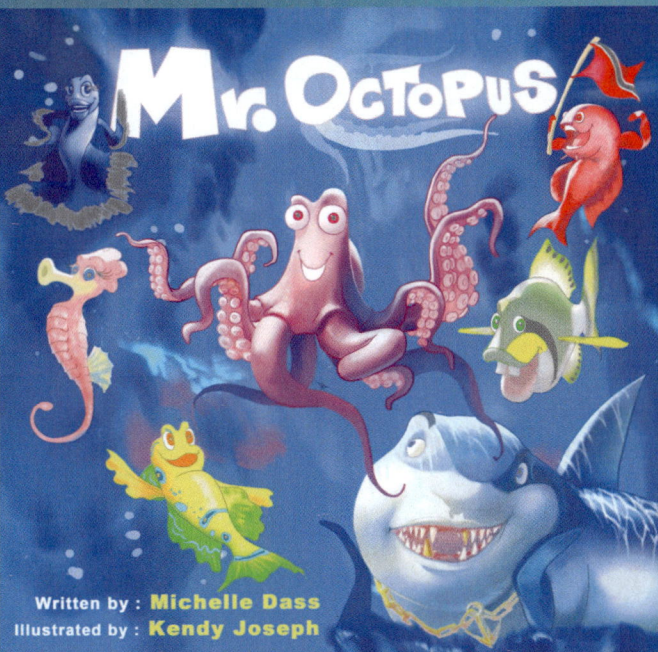

Social Media
@islandkidsbooks

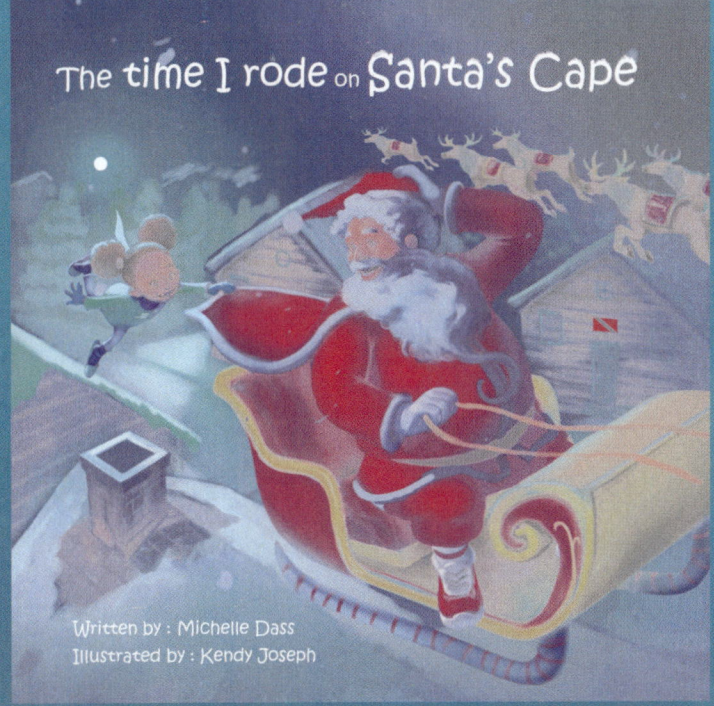

Made in the USA
Las Vegas, NV
23 January 2024

84753087R00024